The Opening of the Field

ALSO BY ROBERT DUNCAN

Heavenly City, Earthly City
Medieval Scenes
Poems 1948-49
Song of the Borderguard
Fragments of a Disordered Devotion
Faust Foutu
Caesar's Gate
Letters (poems 1953-56)
Selected Poems
The Opening of the Field
Roots and Branches
Bending the Bow
Ground Work: Before the War
Fictive Certainties

ABOUT ROBERT DUNCAN

Robert Duncan: Scales of the Marvelous
(Edited by Robert J. Bertholf and Ian W. Reid)

Title page especially designed for the author by Jess

The Opening of the Field

by Robert Duncan

A New Directions Book

Library of Congress Catalog Card Number: 72-93976

(ISBN: 0-8112-0480-4)

Some of these poems first appeared in the following periodicals: *Noonday Review*, *Measure*, *Ark*, *Evergreen Review*, *Botteghe Oscure*, *Trobar*, *Big Table*, *The Nation*, *Foot*, *Poetry*, *Chicago Review*, *Score*, *Folio*, *Chelsea Review*, and *Quixote*.

First published by Grove Press in 1960
First published as New Directions Paperbook 356 in 1973
Published simultaneously in Canada by Penguin Books Canada Limited
Manufactured in the United States of America
New Directions books are printed on acid-free paper

FOURTH PRINTING

Contents

OFTEN I AM PERMITTED TO RETURN TO A MEADOW

as if it were a scene made-up by the mind,
that is not mine, but is a made place,

that is mine, it is so near to the heart,
an eternal pasture folded in all thought
so that there is a hall therein

that is a made place, created by light
wherefrom the shadows that are forms fall.

Wherefrom fall all architectures I am
I say are likenesses of the First Beloved
whose flowers are flames lit to the Lady.

She it is Queen Under The Hill
whose hosts are a disturbance of words within words
that is a field folded.

It is only a dream of the grass blowing
east against the source of the sun
in an hour before the sun's going down

whose secret we see in a children's game
of ring a round of roses told.

Often I am permitted to return to a meadow
as if it were a given property of the mind
that certain bounds hold against chaos,

that is a place of first permission,
everlasting omen of what is.

from its dancers circulates among the other
dancers. This
would-have-been feverish cool excess of
movement makes
each man hit the pitch co-
ordinate.

Lovely their feet pound the green solid meadow.
The dancers
mimic flowers – root stem stamen and petal
our words are,
our articulations, our
measures.

It is the joy that exceeds pleasure.

You have passd the count, she said

or I understood from her eyes. Now
old Friedl has grown so lovely in my years,

I remember only the truth.
I swear by my yearning.

You have conquerd the yearning, she said
The numbers have enterd your feet

turn turn turn

When you're real gone, boy, sweet boy ..

Where have I gone, Beloved?

Into the Waltz, Dancer.

Lovely our circulations sweeten the meadow.
In Ruben's riotous scene the May dancers teach us our learning
seeks abandon!

Maximus calld us to dance the Man.
We calld *him* to call
season out of season-

d mind!

Lovely
join we to dance green to the meadow.

Whitman was right. Our names are left
like leaves of grass,
likeness and liking, the human greenness

tough as grass that survives cruelest seasons.

I see now a radiance.
The dancers are gone.
They lie in heaps, exhausted,
dead tired we say.
They'll sleep until noon.

But I returned early
for the silence,
for the lovely pang that is
a flower,
returnd to the silent dance-ground.

(That was my job that summer. I'd dance until three, then up to get the hall swept before nine – beer bottles, cigarette butts, paper mementos of the night before. Writing it down now, it is the aftermath, the silence, I remember, part of the dance too, an articulation of the time of dancing . . like the almost dead sleeping is a step. I've got it in a poem, about Friedl, moaning in the depths of. But that was another room that summer. Part of my description. What I see is a meadow . .

I'll slip away before they're up . .

and see the dew shining.

from which flow destructions of the Constitution.
No nation stands unstirrd
in whose courts. *I, John, testify:*
I saw. But he who judges must
    know mercy
as a man knows a woman
    in marriage,

for She is fair, whom we, masters, serve.

The Which, says John Adams,
    "requires the continual exercise of virtue
    "beyond the reach
    "of human infirmity, even in its best estate."

Responsibility is to keep
    the ability to respond.
The myriad of spiders' eyes that Rexroth saw
    reflecting light
are glamorless, are testimony
    clear and true.

The shaman sends himself
The universe is filld with eyes then, intensities,
    with intent,
    outflowings of good or evil,
    benemaledictions of the dead,

    but
the witness brings self up before the Law.
It is the Law before the witness that
    makes Justice.

There is no touch that is not each
    to each   reciprocal.

The scale of five, eight, or twelve tones
    performs a judgment
previous to music. The music restores
    health to the land.

The land? The Boyg
in Peer Gynt speaks.
On the stage it was shown: a moving obscurity.

I try to read you, lad, who offer no text.
Not terror now, dumb grief it is,
diabolus – but little devils
are garbled men that speak garble.
Your chosen place is less than hell,
nor hate nor love breeds. There,
disorder is not, order is not, not no
even simpleton need demands my ear.

Hear!

Hear! Beautiful damnd man that lays down his law lays down
himself creates hell
a sentence unfolding healthy heaven.

Thou wilt not allow the suns to move
nor man to mean desire move,
nor rage for war and wine,
here where the mind nibbles,
nor embrace the law under which you lie,
that will not fall upon your face
or upon knees, all
but twisted out of shape, crippled
by angelic Syntax.

Look! the Angel that made a man of Jacob
made Israël in His embrace

was the Law, was Syntax.

Him I love is major mover.

THE STRUCTURE OF RIME I

I ask the unyielding Sentence that shows Itself forth in the language as I make it,

> Speak! For I name myself your master, who come to serve.
> Writing is first a search in obedience.

There is a woman who resembles the sentence. She has a place in memory that moves language. Her voice comes across the waters from a shore I don't know to a shore I know, and is translated into words belonging to the poem:

> *Have heart,* the text reads,
> *you that were heartless.*
> *Suffering joy or despair*
> *you will suffer the sentence*
> *a law of words moving*
> *seeking their right period.*

I saw a snake-like beauty in the living changes of syntax.

> *Wake up,* she cried.
> *Jacob wrestled with Sleep — you who fall into Nothingness and dread sleep.*
> *He wrestled with Sleep like a man reading a strong sentence.*

I will not take the actual world for granted, I said.

> *Why not?* she replied.
> *Do I not withhold the song of birds from you?*
> *Do I not withhold the penetrations of red from you?*
> *Do I not withhold the weight of mountains from you?*
> *Do I not withhold the hearts of men from you?*
>
> *I alone long for your demand.*
> *I alone measure your desire.*

O Lasting Sentence,
sentence after sentence I make in your image. In the feet that measure the dance of my pages I hear cosmic intoxications of the man I will be.

Cheat at this game? she cries.
The world is what you are.
  Stand then
so I can see you, a fierce destroyer of images.

Will you drive me to madness
  only there to know me?
vomiting images into the place of the Law!

THE STRUCTURE OF RIME II

What of the Structure of Rime? I said.

The Messenger in guise of a Lion roard: *Why does man retract his song from the impoverishd air? He brings his young to the opening of the field. Does he so fear beautiful compulsion?*

I in the guise of a Lion roard out great vowels and heard their amazing patterns.

A lion without disguise said: He that sang to charm the beasts was false of tongue. There is a melody within this surfeit of speech that is most man.

What of the Structure of Rime? I asked.

An absolute scale of resemblance and disresemblance establishes measures that are music in the actual world.

The Lion in the Zodiac replied:

The actual stars moving are music in the real world. This is the meaning of the music of the spheres.

A POEM SLOW BEGINNING

remembering powers of love
        and of poetry,
the Berkeley we believed
        grove of Arcady –

that there might be
        potencies in common things,
"princely manipulations of the real"

the hard electric lights,
        filaments exposed
we loved by or studied by,
        romantic,
fused between glare and seraphic glow,
        old lamps of wisdom
        old lamps of suffering .

but that's not the way I saw.
        Crossd,
the sinister eye sees the near
        as clear fact,
                                the far
blurs; the right eye
        fuses all that is
immediate to sight.

                        There first I knew
the companions name themselves
        and move
in time of naming upward
        toward outward
forms of desire and enlightenment,

but intoxicated,
        only by longing
belonging to that first company
of named stars that in heaven
call attention to a tension
        in design,
                                compel

as the letters by which we spell words compel
        magic refinements;

and sought from tree and sun, from night and sea,
old powers — Dionysus in wrath, Apollo in rapture,
Orpheus in song, and Eros secretly

four that Christ-crossd in one Nature
Plato named the First Beloved

that now I see
in all certain dear contributor
        to my being

has given me house, ghost,
image and color,   in whom I dwell
        past Arcady.

For tho Death is sweet   and veriest
        imitator of ecstasy
and there be a Great Lover,
        Salvator Mundi,
whose kingdom hangs above me;

tho the lamps strung among
        shadowy foliage are there;
tho all earlier ravishings,
        raptures,
happend, and sing melodies, moving thus
        when I touch them;

such sad lines they may have been
that now thou hast lifted to gladness.

Of all fearless happiness
from which reaches my life I sing —

        the years radiating

toward the so-calld first days,
toward the so-calld last days,

        inadequate boundaries

of the heart you hold to.

THE STRUCTURE OF RIME III

Glare-eyed Challenger! serpent-skin-coated
accumulus of my days!
Swung in your arms, I grow old.

The numbers swing me. The days that count
my dervish-invisible that time is
up – My time is up?

Period by period the sentences are bound.
Fragments deliverd up
to what celestial timekeeper?

Twice he saw an orange snake that reard up and
spread his hood, cobra-wise.
The orange color does not hold
when the skin is workd. Summer advances
preparing new orange.

The human hood spread orange in time,
fixation of relentless color
– character, scaly-featherd presumption.

After a shower, the mirror
shows the body spreading, orange in time,
reveals accumulations
of my uses, beyond all earliness,

that I bring up to my time,
whatever the pretense,
to this
rearing up
this

snake stance.

THE STRUCTURE OF RIME IV

O Outrider!

when you come to the threshold of the stars,
to the door beyond which moves celestial terror –

the kin at the hearth, the continual cauldron that feeds forth the earth, the heart that comes into being through the blood, the householder among his familiar animals, the beloved turning to his beloved in the dark

create love as the leaves
create from the light life
and return to the remote precincts where the courageous move ramifications of the unknown that appear as trials.

The Master of Rime, time after time, came down the arranged ladders of vision or ascended the smoke and flame towers of the opposite of vision, into or out of the language of daily life, husband to one word, wife to the other, breath that leaps forward upon the edge of dying.

Thus I said to the source of my happiness, I will return. From the moment of your love eternity expands, and you are mere man.

water fire earth and air
all that simple elements were

guardians are.

Among the bleeding branches I hear sentences of my soliloquy. Have you heard the broken limbs of the world-tree knocking, knocking? Here, joy is sternest accuser, a fire that tortures the wet wood.

I tried to die, one wretched voice declared. *There is no death. I left my body hanging behind me, I sought the void. My body hangs before me, immortal image. Men still remember. Their prayers rise from the ground and hold me to the everlasting promise, to the Adam!*

Obsessd poet! another cried. *Your desire devours my heart, a rat tearing at its mate in the rubble of the world. Let us go! The giant Adam must not awaken, for he would claim even* our *ravaged bodies from the consuming black.*

Do you not see that dread as well as joy lights the lamps of his uplifted form? stretchd upon a geometry that rips the wounds from which, black blood, we flow?

The Geometry, I saw, oblivious, knew what? of these sunderings? arranged its sentences intolerant of black or white.

No! No! Say that there are two *worlds*, a man declared. *I shot half my head away.*

A woman cried, *No! There is but one. I live in* one *world, and it is black.*

My soul, the man said, *swings on hinges of destroyd face. Have you not seen Yggdrasill, the Abattoir? The human meat is hanging from every bough. Have you no pity that you count the days of Man?*

You took my life, the woman said. *You will not let me die. Your aroused fire leaves shadows in my heart that whisper to the black into which I go.*

The old women came from their caves to close the too many doors that lead into pastures. Thru which the children pass, and in the high grass build their rooms of green, kingdoms where they dwell under the will of grasshopper, butterfly, snail, quail, thrush, mole and rabbit.

Old Woman, your eye searches the field like a scythe! The riches of the living green lie prepared for your store. Ah, but you come so near to the children! you have almost returnd to them. Their voices float up from their faraway games where. The tunneld grass hides their clearings. Swords and blades cut the near blue of sky. Their voices surround you.

Old Woman, at last you have come so near you almost understand them.

Have you recalld then how the soul floats as the tiger-tongued butterfly or that sapphire, the humming-bird, does, where it will?

Lying in the grass, the world was all of the field, and I saw a kite on its string, tugging, bounding – far away as my grandmother – dance against the blue from its tie of invisible delight.

In the caves of blue within the blue the grandmothers bound, on the brink of freedom, to close the too many doors from which the rain falls.

Thus, the grass must give up new keys to rescue the living.

THE STRUCTURE OF RIME VII

Black King Glélé dwells in the diabolical, a tranquil spirit of pure threat, an orb radiating the quiet pool, the black water, to the boundaries of his image. Solitary among demons, he appears to them and to us demonic. We have composed him over again of enlarged terror – claws, teeth, hair, eyes, mouth, broodings of flesh, corruptions of blood, pustulences, wounds, irruptions, horn, bone, gristle, calcifications, scarrings.

These are the counsels of the Wood:

> *Lie down, Man, under Love. The streams of the Earth seek passage thru you, tree that you are, toward a foliage that breaks at the boundaries of known things. The measures of Man are outfoldings of Chaos. In the Dance you turn from your steps cross visibly thru the original mess – messages of created music, imprints, notes, chosen scales, lives, gestures. Look behind you, courageous traveler! you will see that past where you have never been. See! these are not* your *footprints that fall from your feet.*

And I stand, stranger to tranquility because I am enamord of song, to sing to Glélé the King as I would sing to relentless history.

> *I am like the century's tree given over to new leaves.*
> *I am like the bird of the season restraind to his piping.*
> *I am like the Fire that Heraclitus tells us is*
> *kindled in measure, quenchd in measure.*

The Rime falls in the outbreakings of speech as the Character falls in the act wherefrom life springs, footfalls in Noise which we do not hear but see as a Rose pushd up from the stem of our longing.

The kindled image remains that we calld a Rose. Glélé torn up from what we calld suffering answers:

> *I am the Rose.*

THREE PAGES FROM A BIRTHDAY BOOK

The almost-not-believed Moon moved in ghost among the things we are made to believe or make to believe. *I was once Great Artemis* she whisperd. *I was once Madam Moon in full. But let me join the toys to hang in the window of Make Believe, for ride through the years we must by whatever ruse.*

. .

In the passion of the Unicorn, believing, he laid himself down to the White Lady's lap. The Butcher's men came then and slaughterd the heavy beast, Whose near-sighted eyes held to the Lady's dreamy eyes, fixd without flicker, most foreign. Because of the blood, the flayd flesh, the brutality, we picture (instead of the true monoceros, occult and impure) the white innocence of a fairy horse, of the crownd animal hero.

. . .

Thoth, stern Master of the Soul, came to weigh the birthday toys. So many amulets the Soul had gatherd! little guardians of our delight, frivolities.

What frivolities have you gatherd against the Night? the Spirit of the Night askd.

Friends bring their fondness to stand like a little army against a great army. Each birthday present presents a wish, an allegiance to stand in place of the birth night.

The day nursery is wisely prepared thus by its nurses each morning for the nursery of the night, in order that green shoots of a child inhabit the dark of man.

Go, then, with only a blessing, into the Pit, Joseph! And the Brothers (friends) return with your many-colord Coat, torn, like a wish ravaged by Beasts of the Field.

The little night-lights, the wishes, released, disappear—balloons cut from their strings by the Judge's kind hand.

In the destruction of all pleasures the Consul of the Dead delivers the Child at last into his cloud of joy.

might have been.
Certainly these ashes might have been pleasures.
Pilgrims on their way to the Holy Places remark
this place. Isn't it plain to all
that these mounds were palaces? This was once
a city among men, a gathering together of spirit.
It was measured by the Lord and found wanting.

It was measured by the Lord and found wanting,
destroyd by the angels that inhabit longing.
Surely this is Great Sodom where such cries
as if men were birds flying up from the swamp
ring in our ears, where such fears that were once
desires walk, almost spectacular,
stalking the desolate circles, red eyed.

This place rumord to have been a City surely was,
separated from us by the hand of the Lord.
The devout have laid out gardens in the desert,
drawn water from springs where the light was blighted.
How tenderly they must attend these friendships
or all is lost. All *is* lost.
Only the faithful hold this place green.

Only the faithful hold this place green
where the crown of fiery thorns descends.
Men that once lusted grow listless. A spirit
wrappd in a cloud, ashes more than ashes,
fire more than fire, ascends.
Only these new friends gather joyous here,
where the world like Great Sodom lies under fear.

The world like Great Sodom lies under Love
and knows not the hand of the Lord that moves.
This the friends teach where such cries
as if men were birds fly up from the crowds
gatherd and howling in the heat of the sun.
In the Lord Whom the friends have named at last Love
the images and loves of the friends never die.

This place rumord to have been Sodom is blessd
in the Lord's eyes.

THE BALLAD OF THE ENAMORD MAGE

How the Earth turns round under the Sun I know,
And how the Numbers in the Constellations glow,
How all Forms in Time will grow
And return to their single Source
Informd by Grief, Joy, insatiable Desire
And cold Remorse.

Serpents I have seen bend the Evening Air
Where Flowers that once Men and Women were
Voiceless spread their innocent Lustre.
I have seen green Globes of Water
Enter the Fire. In my Sight
Tears have drownd the Flames of Animal Delight.

I, a poor writer, who knows not
where or wherefor my body was begot.

In a World near a City in a green Tree
I was once a Bird shot down by Thee.
And Thou, Beloved, shot from Thy young Bow
An Arrow from which my Blood doth daily flow
And stoppd the Song
That now I sing Thee all Night long.

I, turning my verse, waiting for the rime,
that know not the meaning of my name.

In a place where a Stone was, hot in the Sun,
I was once a Mage, dry as a Bone,
And calld to me a Demon of myself alone
Who from my Thirst conjured a green River
And out of my Knowledge I saw Thee run,
A Spring of pure Water.

I, late at night, facing the page
writing my fancies in a literal age.

How all beings into all beings pass,
How the great Beasts eat the human Grass,
And the Faces of Men in the World's Glass
Are faces of Apes, Birds, Diamonds,
Worlds and insubstantial Shapes
Conjured out of the Dust – Alas!
These things I know.
Worlds out of Worlds in Magic grow.

I, mortal, that live by chance,
and know not why you love,
praise the great wheel where the spirits dance,
for by your side I move.

THE BALLAD OF MRS NOAH

Mrs Noah in the Ark
wove a great nightgown out of the dark,
did Mrs Noah,

had her own hearth in the Holy Boat,
two cats, two books, two cooking pots,
had Mrs. Noah,

two pints of porter, two pecks of peas,
and a stir in her stew of memories.

Oh, that was a town, said Mrs Noah,
that the Lord in His wrath
did up and drown!

I liked its windows and I liked its trees.
Save me a little, Lord, I prayd on my knees.
And now, Lord save me, I've two of each!
apple, apricot, cherry and peach.

How shall I manage it? I've two of them all –
hairy, scaly, leathery, slick,

fluttery, buttery, thin and thick,
shaped like a stick, shaped like a ball,
too tiny to see, and much too tall.

I've all that I askd for and more and more,
windows and chimneys, and a great store
of needles and pins, of outs and ins,
and a regular forgive-us for some of my sins.

She wove a great nightgown out of the dark
decorated like a Sunday Park
with clouds of black thread to remember her grief
sewn about with bright flowers to give relief,

and, in a grim humor, a border all round
with the little white bones of the wicked drownd.

Tell me, Brother, what do you see?
said Mrs Noah to the Lowly Worm.

O Mother, the Earth is black, black.
To my crawlly bride and lowly me
the Earth is bitter as can be
where the Dead lie down and never come back,
said the blind Worm.

Tell me, Brother, what do *you* see?
said Mrs Noah to the sleeping Cat.

O Mother, the weather is dreadful wet.
I'll keep house for you wherever you'll be.
I'll sit by the fireside and be your pet.
And as long as I'm dry I'll purr for free,
said snug-loving Cat.

Tell me, Brother, has the Flood gone?
said Mrs Noah to the searching Crow.

No. No. No home in sight.
I fly thru the frightful waste alone,
said the carrion Crow.
The World is an everlasting Night.

Now that can't be true, Noah, Old Noah,
said the good Housewife to her good Spouse.
How long must we go in this floating House?
growing old and hope cold,
Husband, without new land?

And then Glory-Be with a Rainbow to-boot!
the Dove returnd with an Olive Shoot.

Tell me, Brother, what have we here,
my Love? to the Dove said Mrs Noah.

It's a Branch of All-Cheer
you may wear on your nightgown all the long year
as a boa, Mrs Noah, said the Dove,
with God's Love!

    Then out from the Ark
    in her nightgown all dark
    with only her smile to betoken the Day
    and a wreath-round of olive leaves

Mrs Noah steppd down
into the same old wicked repenting
Lord-Will-We-Ever recently recoverd
comfortable World-Town.

O where have you been, Mother Noah, Mother Noah?

I've had a great Promise for only Tomorrow.
In the Ark of Sleep I've been on a sail
over the wastes of the world's sorrow.

And the Promise? the Tomorrow? Mother Noah, Mother Noah?

Ah! the Rainbow's awake
and we will not fail!

we consider
precedent to that Shekinah, She
in whom the Jew has his communion.
Lovely to look at, modesty
imparts to her nakedness willowy
grace. Bright with spring, *vestita*
di nobilissimo colore umile ed onesto sanguigno
Dante saw her *so that the heart trembled.*
In Hell Persephone showd
brightness of death her face, spring
slumbering.
Came to that spring,
or is attendant there, to draw water:
thus, Rachel, *dal principio del suo anno nono,*
a girl, lifted to Jacob's dry mouth
her cup that fed his manhood's thirst.
Because we thirst for clarity,
the crystal clear brook Undine wakes
unquenchable longing, in which
jewels innocent show in lovely depths.

Her persistence makes
Freud's teaching that a child has sexual phantasies
terrible. Yellowy green that breaks winter
of daffodil or asphodel, witch's color
(but to Wordsworth's natural heart epiphany)
Ophelia wore, heart's rendering.
Hamlet, Edith Sitwell tells us was dark earth, cries
"Get thee to a nunnery!" Ophelia grieves
for her dead Father, the old year
thrown aside. "The little Fertility ghost or Vegetation demon,
ghost of Spring, casts herself into the stream
wreathed with flowers." Another maiden,
Elizabeth Eleanor Siddal in a silvery dress
"drowning for an hour or so" posed for Millais
to capture a wild chastity. And Bonnard
teaches us again and again where she appears

reflecting watery blues and greens in tiled bathrooms
a wife may be   maiden to the eye.

No goddess, She
must be revived,
Cora among the grasses.
Hearts
revive with her.

Memory
holds particular maidens
inviolate
and quickens
as if Spring had arrived

when in an elderly maiden's face
(Marianne Moore's)
the camera shows
a penetrating beauty
and Her grace.

The old say they are young in heart.   Youth
is part of power in the thriving shoot
the earnest begonia forces toward the sun.
When illness overtook her, Mrs Adam
dwelt in her girlhood and heard
music from a piano that was not here,
strains of sixty years ago.
Her mind was wandering.   It is well
of water we return to.

Men have mothers.   They are of women born
and from this womanly knowledge
womanly, but Christ
was more and rare that was a maiden's Babe:
He was part girl.   He had solitude.

Because it is Mystery, such puberty
counterfeited in simpering coy glances, piety,
giggles, girlish attitudes,
is loathsome, contaminated water, field
desecrated by picnickers.

It is the girl the man knows nothing of.
His heart stops short and must
belong to her by trust he knows as pain:
 — *quando m'apparve Amor subitamente,*
thus Dante Alighieri gaind New Life,
therein Love apprehended. "The pain of loving you,"
Lawrence writes, "is almost more than I can bear . . .
I live in fear." *Donna della salute!*

Fear is a flame in your propriety.

The Close

Close to her construct I pace the line,
the containd homage arranged, reflections
on Marianne Moore's natural style, an artifice
where sense may abound. As in a photograph of her
I found the photographer with his camera had caught
artfully a look where this flame took my mind
of beauty in which a maiden's
unlikely hardihood may be retaind.

THE PROPOSITIONS

1

SKILL

the precision the hand knows
necessary to operate.
The incisive line contains this study, releases search.
Ocean seeks verification–attack, retreat.
These passions of the moon define
shore lines.
Dr Sea seeks whatever variations from prescribed course.
He comes to life (to focus)
in recognitions hand, eye, ear (gravity
he needs) prepared for.

The poem
suggests skill is not sufficient. How
the masterly physician excites our admiration!
Steeld against seductive ruin he
is impersonal. But look,
the blotchd face of bloat and bladder.
from which eyes
that have shied from death,
precision, study put together.

How vitally we desired disaster and could not
in the play manage to show
the vomiting blood, the retch necessary
to befoul love, study, the lines.
As I wanted her on the stage, wet with it.

Does the moon move violent imperatives,
such responsibilities that Dr Sea might
cut wild, hack away,
splay open the face to give those eyes
sufficient deformity to face life
expressively?
hack away the offending flesh if need be?

Out of the golden field the black crows fly
to Van Gogh's black blood.

Artaud
goes thru humiliating poses of crisis
before he realizes madness. O
shall I never wear the contemptuous crown
that scorns affection
and woos awareness in catastrophe?

This skill
at home in violence did not flinch
as we would have
lost stomach. In the surgical ward I walkd
—eyes averted
from the fact, a face too real.
But Dr Sea
sewd it up, didn't he? Made a mouth
any how.
Ow ugh a-a-a- it said.

The cook with Old Man River
and some blowsy female went on a drunk
and ends up in 14-A
the Freestone Mansion Rooms. The moon-
shine turns rot-gut
at the bed where Old Man River roars he'll have her
and she, wretched,
whimpers. For catastrophe was there. Where?
Quick! the cook
slips the lady out the door and
Old Man River with straightedge razor
slits him open incisive
from back the ear to thigh in one
swipe. Fate strikes
where we thot to escape. The blood
ready to escape,
to be free!

Cook was there, made O.K. In a month
the nerve ends Dr Sea rejoind
will grow and heal. The skill
must wait for all

to grow together.   It is a gathering of crows,
    omens, that animates the artifice.
How awe-full that other, the patchd face
    (I would have ended it!)
rank growth, a life   triumphant
    that demolishes skill.

    Dr Sea must go on. He demands
cosmetic tortures now to shape some
    deceptive shore line.
                                But the eyes
flinch, and Blubber Puss holds out.
    Don't do no more to me!

Doesn't he care?   Who?
where?   mangled his face?

did he . . .?

            Another cook   on board ship
sliced his head from neck   having set
            the electric meat saw
to work. The crew was sick
            and could not   face food.

    A categorical imperative!

Enlightenment revolted by unreason
    waited for the bloody mob

    to rise. Or (1890)
"nothing else in the world but murder and death"
    aesthetic author of *News From Nowhere*
William Morris saw preceded
    return to the field.   He
who thot that perfect love would know
    jealousy   courteously,
preferring dis-ease   to rage.

                        Out
under the moon   the man goes,
                                        animal ocean.

Skill rises, a sensibility, a
discrimination.

How many books did Dr Sea consume?
The Teaching guides his hand–restrains
accident
imperative.

He cuts the meat but sees

anatomies.

2

LOVE then:

might I deny the force that drove me to the ground
prime reality?

Have you never come to grief
in which love holds reciprocal pain
of heart? Tears

in natural flood that verifies?
The sexual drive, erect
intention, is deep, is absolute.
No more deep or absolute

than tenderness. It is life
that tenders green shoots of
hurt and healing we name Love.

In the dream the Masters of Cruelty gave me
the choice: Shall we
tear out *your* eyes . . . or *his?*

"No! No, tear out *my* eyes." But what is terror?
It flows both ways.
I saw their trap. I did not dare
see *his* pain, and askd him
to bear with me.

"No. *His.*" Is this
hidden in blind Love?

Joy too we share   perilously.

Or are you so confident in pleasure you forget wholeness of experience?

The agony he felt was for *me*.   We
could not disguise the absolute
sentences of pain that wrackd him.

I could not let him go free then
into his own pain. But be- longing
claimd the seeing it thru.

The Crown the King wears, Reciprocity
is not actual.
Love prospers in right reason, but in season

has rigorous roots in romantic legend,
fulsomely   to
"row on Moonmere," obey
the pull of magic stones, dream
associations, scriptures out of god-intoxications,
weirds, returns . . .

The comfortable hearth-fire warms because of warnings.
"In sickness and in health"   health
not easier . . . Are there
delicate adjustments? not to acclaim
or restrain. The signature must be admired.

Olson names Love one of four qualities.   What
sensations prosper in the good?

Pain, pleasure,   in this focus
we hold to the condition.

The qualities as we know them in-
form demand.

And for Love   I stand   perilously.

"*He* knows better," Freud said,
meaning the cock   gives his own condition.

But the sick Knight of the (Heart)

followd the white Hart into its wilderness.
    "In sickness and in . . ." the Land
that is Health   blighted
    everywhere
troubled by insistent Falseness

        that threw up Knights and Demoiselles
        that did desire the Heart to eat
        that brought grief to Fair Things
        that hid great Wealth beneath its Hill.

Nietzsche's portrait where all has fallen into the black
I hang upon my wall.

    Love sets its triumphs in the void,
        commands the real.

3

This is THE SENDING OUT.

I see the tree.   It changes.   Mineral
    vegetable   animal.   Of generations.
It exceeds me.

                Come back. Come back.
Tell us of excess.
    What was the sign that limited?

Do not serve the tree.
This is the sending.

This place is litterd with great stones.

    No more!   Return to the shore
we remember.   Do not go beyond our knowledge.

    Bring back that black thing.
    we did not have in our story.
    It alone to speak, to give strangeness.

    .

In the field of the poem   the unexpected
    must come.

We wait.
It does not come.

There is a disturbance in the House.
I had forgotten its orders. The plants
ask to be waterd.

If we have not set things to rights,
the indwelling
is not with us, there are no instructions.

4

THE SPIDER'S SONG
FROM FILAMENT OF HIS LOVE SENT OUT
(memoria Whitman)

O gorgeous Blue Bottle!
What raptures your wild struggle!
tremblings of the veil,
shakings of the center!

5

THE KEEPING

I would bring my life complete before you,
have given it earnest discriminations,
discoverd its keeping, its natural boundaries,
named the good Good, the evil Evil.

I would not confuse the elements.
It is from longing my making proceeds.

When I summon intellect it is to the melody
of this longing. Thy hand,
Beloved, restores
the chords of this longing.
Here, in this thirst that defines Beauty,
I have found kin.

Nerves tremble upon its reaches.
Sinews of the act have tone under its laws.
What I call magic proceeds from the heart:
        the blood there in its courses
has pulse in this longing. O melody
immaculately carrying pulses of this longing!

What opulence of my temper does not advance its charges?
What intricate shifting of mood in the world's weather

does not show cosmic affinities? The light
out of which the manifest flows
        goes by this longing.

O poet! if you would share my way,
come in under the Law, the great Longing.
Dwell, as the guardian plant does, by appetite
at the shores of the Sun, come
        under the Moon, keep
                secret allegiance to the out-pouring stars
                        in Night's courts,

move into the Dance   Whose bonds men hold
    holy :   the Light

life lights in like eyes.

By magic we may arise and speak with spirits without knowing ourselves

FOUR PICTURES OF THE REAL UNIVERSE

THE GATE

O Lords of Intensity, initiates of catastrophe:
the star observed by Tycho Brahe in 1572
visible in bright daylight, the star
recorded by Chinese astronomers in the year
1054, the Star of our Lord . . .
        into the holocausts of helium
the ravenous spirit sends out its hunters.

The Queen that dwells in the dark
feeds on the death of stars, devours
emanations out of light perishing.

THE WALL

Crownd Beast of Pure Thriving!
You pass thru the wall of thot,
thru the stone wall, thru the walls of the body,
gathering all into your strength,
altering nothing.

From your roar, legions fly thru the universe
ringing the suns, sounding flames of immediate victory
that we see as white flowers
lost in the waves of morning green.

THE PASTURE

The Great Sun Himself comes
to eat at my heart, asks
that I return myself into Him.

And the white body, a Moon,
in the precincts of the Earth revolves.
How the Dead draw the Sea after them!

But the Living, the immortal corpuscles
sail without shadow
toward the pyres of the Sun.

THE CLOSET

And does not the spirit attend secretly
the music that is hidden away from me,
chords that hold the stars in their courses,
outfoldings of sound from the seed of first light?

Were it not for the orders of music hidden
we should be claimd by the preponderant void.

EVOCATION

At the dance of the Hallows I will tell my love.
There where the threshers move,
the lewdness of women ripening the wheat,
the men in the outer room joking,
how the Holy moves over them!

The Earth shakes. Kore! Kore! (for
I was thinking of her – She
who shakes the stores of ancestral grain)
The Earth does not shake again. Troubled,
the heart recovers. But is moved.
At the dance of the Hallows I will tell my love.
It moves to fill with song, with wine,
the trouble, the quiet, the cup, that follows
the divine Threshers.

Kore! O visage as of sun-glare, thunderous
    awakener, light treader!
will you not wake us again? shake the earth under us?

At the dance of the Hallows I will tell my love.
It is my song of the whole year I sing
rendering lovely the fall of Her feet
and there where Her feet spring, even
at the dance of the Hallows I will tell my love,
the melody from whose abundance leaps
the slow rounds of winter, pounds summer's heat.

How the Holy moves over them I will tell my love
that lies a grain among the living grain.
Therefore I join them, dancing, dancing . . .
a thresher among the Threshers. Kore! Kore!
(for I was thinking of her when the quake came,
    of radiant desire underground)
Thou hast my heart, a grain, in the Earth's store.

At the dance of the Hallows I praise thee therefore,
    Earth-mover, tender Thresher,
    Queen of our dance-floor!

OF BLASPHEMY

If you have not entered the Dance, you mistake the event.

— ST. JOHN AT EPHESUS

The angel who is (Lord of) Fortune (*but there is a pun here: he is also Lord of the Spokes of the Wheel or Spokesman*) . . . we came to a place where the grass was burnt back. "Look!" (I was commanded) . . . And leaning into the blasphemer's face I saw that it was Man's face. "The grass does not appear here, for he has blasted his sight." . . . he gives . . . (the Angel) opend a door of the world's misery (*again there is a possible pun: by lengthening the vowel of the verb* opend-a-door *we may read* turnd, *and by a like shift* misery *becomes* wheel) "That string," the Angel said, "runs thru the harp of the world as does the string of your joy. There is a strand of the blasphemy in the harp of generations from which man needs daring to play the full music." The musicker (pickd at) his solitary (string) . . . "He brays" (the Angel said) "against his own false image, for he does not know of the Great Music and thinks he strikes at the heart of the Universe . . . He *strikes* at the heart of the Universe!"

For until you call yourself my own, I shall not be what I am.

— ST. JOHN AT EPHESUS

NOR IS THE PAST PURE.

The realized
is dung of the ground that feeds us, rots,
falls apart

into the false,
displaying wounds of the pure
urge, mounds
mulch for covetous burrowing thought.

But from time's rot
it is toward another time we keep our root
known.

For the Lover
that all lovers perform
claps His hands and dismisses
corruption, for the innocence of the act,
for the heart's preparation.

Praise then the hand that moves to deliver
– this, this too, the forbidden act –
to the upgiving,
to intimations of the secret Mover.

Which we are not permitted without corruption.

O happy actor
who in the offices of self seeks
that which prospers:

the full burgeoning, ripeness that is ready,
the generous falling
into the raptures of heroic death, the ground,
the mulch, the right furrow.

Satan that was once great Pluto underground!
And we came up out of a dark hole
into All Night of the World. Do we
not remember centuries of the cold?
Did we not, children, cry for a comforter,
came to a no place we knew where we were
and saw in the distance, indistinct,
the Hornd Master
tending the fires that surrounded His field,

that was once great Fear
setting His bountiful garden, He
our Boundary-Stone, our
Lord of the Marches that devour Chaos.

O seed occult we planted in the dark furrow!
O potency we rested and coverd over!
O life thriving lightwards, gathering strength!
The image of our longing is the full head of seed,
the wheat-gold ready

to give in its ripeness (our labors) food
        everlasting!

Again and again return underground
to the dark fires, the Satanic thriving.
The First Prince is of Light ignorant.
        Toward *scientia* he strives.

The Seed evil, the sprouting by desire, the
        shoots of beauty, the flowering art,
the seed good good good, the good ear
        full and ripe, trembling with sound
that joyfull we return to the underground!

Thus the Evil is seed, terror
        held by courage (our labors) nourishd
by devotion (our labors)
        anticipates Beauty.

This is the Book of the Earth, the field of grass
        flourishing.
This is the region that feeds forth souls
        under the old orders
returning to the dominion of its King and Queen.
It is only the midden heap, Beauty: shards,
        scraps of leftover food, rottings,
        the Dump
where we read history, larvae of all dead things,
        mixd seeds, waste, off-castings, despised
        treasure, vegetable putrifactions
        : from this adultery committed,

the plant that provides, Corn
        that at Eleusis Kore brought
out of Hell, health manifest. Heracles said:
        I have seen Kore.
What face more terrible? I am initiate,
        prepared for Hades.
        Queen of the Middenheap I have seen.
Death is prerequisite to the growth of grass.

This is the Book of the Provider.

CROSSES OF HARMONY AND DISHARMONY

1

"Gladly, the cross-eyed bear" – the cross
rising from the eye a strain of visible song
that Ursa Major dances,
star notes, configurations
from right to wrong
the all night long body stretchd bare
sleep's guy in the game of musical shares,

Mizar, Benatnasch at the tail —
sky of hairy distances, male
to the fields of earth beneath night's paw,
female to other orders.

Who was? changed into the bear I saw?
wearing the uncouth skin, unbathed
Old Stinker sweaty with beastly nails.

Wait for me, I said, I'll dance
wherever you are to be to where I am
a round
I'll dance the shambles of the year
round the Christ in the Abattoir.

The Moon looks down
upon the Sun crownd on His tree
with beastly nails and down
upon both you and me.
Shares of the Moon is Man his tree.

2

Across the years each sentence goes.
The poet sends the image of a rose
from its particular fragrance to the sun.
Across the pages of the completed man
tears of "inward performance" run.

The stars through centuries return
rimes of light to burn in this moment's eye
universes that flicker – where?
the sensory line
breaks

so that the lines of the verse do not meet,
imitating that void between
two images of a single rose near at hand, the one
slightly above and to the right . . .

"the double vision
due to maladjustment of the eyes" like
"visual delusions arising from some delirium
illustrates surrounding spatial regions",

"pure mode of presentational immediacy".

3

and from where I was saw
far below in time-swarm man hung
end
parenthesis.

Let
it have no earthly importance.
It is a proposition from which

time flows and takes on umbrage of
ultimate things, trans-
mutations, crossings over,
the tremblings of love.

"There is no impression of law or of lawlessness."

There was no law of Jesus then.
There was
only a desire of savior,
man-gate of God,
a roar of the Holy Sea seeking
lion's mouth

to take the place of placid potencies,
old orders.

It is a proposition that takes from lords
faith's fiefs,
castles emptied by impatient Emperors
from which

time turns, a body burns
new informations at arm's reach,
lure for a more intense feeling.

A bush puts forth roses upon roses
to illustrate the afternoon
abundancies of white, scarlet, yellow –
the beautiful profusion takes me.

Whitehead "may not neglect
the multifariousness of the world –
the fairies dance, and Christ is naild to the cross"

towards fullness:

4

A GROUP OF SONGS FOR AN EVENING'S SING

Who-Do-We-Not-Know-Her sits at the piano.

She knows no improvisations.
And our young voices
sing as she strikes up familiar melodies

stale chords, old chords

that turn the heart toward thots of
parting.

Our voices faltering. Imperfect youth!

that out of tune gives rank satisfaction some refinement of
unease.

A hurdy-gurdy in the streets! In Spring's
bright air we hear her call

Come, Children, see!   the music man
sweet as truth . . . Come see

the monkey dance upon his string   and doff
his hat.

A sentiment.
not to be uprooted! a ground of delight!

Quick, come see! Life trembles,
memory` reaches

and from where I was   saw

A POEM OF DESPONDENCIES

We go whatever route to run un-
    obstructed. A city without seasons
may bug a man who needs thunderstorms,
snow, frost-bitten leaves, to drive away
    stagnant August.

Kêres, dirty little things that fill the air,
    obscure a weather's message.
What softness massage festering reason?

    In Scotland fairies
coverd with hair scare girls and
prepare twisted paths into the mire,
    false landscapes, blight light,
    sour dawn, noon or near night,
to reflect heart's discontent or
    raise vapors from sexual treasure
as gold rots in the ground sprouts fever.

This green is obscene, seeded
    where will moves not, no
    stout stalk leaf of the grass
but the green kêres, in fury, fly
    up from the bog of –
insatiable under the hand urge?

It's the fearful rising where the cock
    won't rise
that sickens the eyes, tricks
    the domestic poseur to self-loathing.
Black bile not blood drips
    from the enclosure.

This is the way the land lies.

As who from dreams as from marsh
    wakes.
They are mosquitoes biting wet flanks
    of natural flesh.

Did you? Did you? Who? opend the damnd
    box? But
I hate locks. I wish I could give you
    such openness,
filths, upswarms of fervor, to hold . . .

A man held so, up-
held we see in staind unmoving
sea moved, sustaind in
Hell,
        mannd against calm.

POETRY, A NATURAL THING

Neither our vices nor our virtues
further the poem. "They came up
and died
just like they do every year
on the rocks."

The poem
feeds upon thought, feeling, impulse,
to breed itself,
a spiritual urgency at the dark ladders leaping.

This beauty is an inner persistence
toward the source
striving against (within) down-rushet of the river,
a call we heard and answer
in the lateness of the world
primordial bellowings
from which the youngest world might spring,

salmon not in the well where the
hazelnut falls
but at the falls battling, inarticulate,
blindly making it.

This is one picture apt for the mind.

A second: a moose painted by Stubbs,
where last year's extravagant antlers
lie on the ground.
The forlorn moosey-faced poem wears
new antler-buds,
the same,

"a little heavy, a little contrived",

his only beauty to be
all moose.

KEEPING THE RHYME

By stress and syllable
by change-rhyme and contour
we let the long line pace even awkward to its period.

The short line
we refine
and keep for candor.

This we remember:
ember of the fire
catches the word if we but hear
    ("We must understand what is happening")
and springs to desire,
a bird-right light
    sound.

This is the Yule-log that warms December.
This is new grass that springs from the ground.

A SONG OF THE OLD ORDER

Sing fair the Lady and her knight.
Sing the two friends, brothers or lovers,
    who keep troth.
And praise, praise,
    the man and the woman
    naked betrothed
who give green to the earth
    and by their love
raise the day's light!

These things we sing fair
    from the earliest time
burnt leaf of november and green of may
    the change of the year,
    the rounds of the moon,
we sing in our measures and
    return with our rime.

For our Lady waxeth and waneth.
    Joan grows sullen
    and Joan delights.
burnt leaf of november and green of may

These things we number
    among our delights:
burnt leaf of november and green of may
    the replenishing work
    and play we devote
to the troth we keep with the source of light
    that is right, right,
as the stars in their courses
    bind the dark.

For our Lord has awakend our hearts.
    John has known grief
    and John's known joy,
burnt leaf of november and green of may.

Know you your Father
 that gave you your name?
burnt leaf of november and green of may.
 O show me, my brother,
 by night and by day
for the way I go is by your side
 the dance whose figures
 may measure man's pride.

For the Lord has redeemd the abyss.
 He gave the new law.
 He sufferd the kiss.
burnt leaf of november and green of may.

These things we adore:
 the bindings of law,
burnt leaf of november and green of may,
 that gives us new courage
 that gave us to love
one in whose likeness we discover the day.

For our Lady gives and returns us.
 She teaches all
 and she hides the key.
burnt leaf of november and green of may

•

Sing fair the Lady and her knight!
Sing the two friends, brothers or lovers,
 who keep troth,
And praise, praise,
 the man and the woman
 naked betrothed
who give green to the earth
 and by their love
raise the day's light!

THE QUESTION

Have you a gold cup
dedicated to thought
that is like clear water
held in a flower?

or sheen of the gold
burnishd on wood
to furnish fire-glow
a burning in sight only?

color of gold, feel of gold
weight of gold? Does the old alchemist
speak in metaphor
of a spiritual splendor?

or does he remember
how that metal is malleable?
chalice workd of gold at the altar,
chasuble elaborated in gold?

in Cuzco llamas of solid gold in the *Inti Pampa*
the Sun's field with Stars, Lightning, Rainbow, Moon
round it? or impounded at Fort Knox?
what wealth without show?

When money at last moves a free medium
using work as measure, justified
to needs man's common nature heeds,
will there be riches for public pleasure?

Will the good metal return
to use? gold leaf to the house roof?
our treasure above ground
sure glow for the eye to see?

For tho *les malades imaginaires*,
who puddle in their psyches
to suck their own bones, declare
lucre is shit,

gold is to the artisan potent
for beauty; and money remains
"the growing grass that can nourish the living sheep",
real only as that manly trust

we know as the field of accumulated good,
the keep
of justice   our labors
that the gold head of the wheat thrive

for the common bread.
Work the old images from the hoard,
el trabajo en oro that gives wealth semblance
and furnishes ground for the gods to flourish.

O have you a service of rich gold
to illustrate the board of public goods?
as in the old days   regalia of gold
to show wherein the spirit had food?

THE PERFORMANCE WE WAIT FOR

        defines us its attendants.
From the images of man
        moves manhood upon us.
Nerves turnd to that tension find
        a binding there,
that gives imperfection reference.

A King — the one we call the Poet —
        under the Crown of an Idea
seeks quiet of a garden
        even be it a single plant,
tended in the evening. Prosper
        O green friend! for I have seen
signature that is ground of all delight
        in the sight of you, that from seed
has given stem, leaves, flower
        of your nature,

that we may not depart from, but have there
    fathering force, a temenos,
bounded by grandparents, that founds
    one field.

And the cross thereof

(north east west south
or name them
four seasons) where

light flows

from fire; desire from agony;
    speech from the tongue tied —
the Word from the hung mind
    moves to Its mouth.

•

The Moon's not come full.
Yet I'll play the amorous fool.
You're too drunk to make it, my lad.
We've no place to go if we're almost there.
Desire has only one house. Your eyes
may catch mine without catching fire.
We strain against tides the stars move
Who are impatient for love.

Who shall I be
that your smile holds me at bay?
You're too driven to make it, my lad.
Your white face fades away from me.
Desire has only one time. Your lips
seek solace, yet find no joy in mine.
Aie! there is no greater wrong
than to force the song.

•

Among the many persons I am
    is Wanderer-To-Come-To-The-Secret-Place-
Where-Waits-The-Discovery-That-Moves-The-Heart.

I rose in a rage last night
potent to melt all the areas of my dream
but the eyes of my beloved met mine
restoring the boundaries of one Me.

O night book! among your pages
is there a chapter calld Many-In-One
Or are you the old deceiver
that shows us fate with many branches?

These things I would record:
the gift of flight
where I am returnd to the element of air
a creature of substance without weight
or, having weight,
solitary skilld denizen of my own nature.

One of my persons is calld Child-Of-The-Wind-Loved-
That-Bends-The-Oak.

O book out of troubled waters written!
scatterd over your surfaces
I have seen notes of stars reflected.

These things I would record:
the drift of sand
at the edge of the sea's eternal roar
where my dry hands impetuous for sound
unlock from keys
inventions from inventions of the world's music
upon a breaking harpsicord.

Have you not heard him?
He-Whose-Eyes-Are-Withheld-From-Tears?

AT CHRISTMAS

In the center of the field   a Lamb
from whose male heart the intellectual blood
      gushes, gushes, gushes
to fill the cup that is now a poem,
      stillness
toward which the procession comes,
      muted
from the world's music as if drawn home.

I had forgotten Him.
The virulent green returning
spears of the Elohim
cut gashes of yearning into song.

From which opening of blood   a woman
in the center of the field disturbs,
      nakedness
we were afraid to touch but were drawn
      into that lust
(for Love has orders within orders)
her breasts redeeming milk to the hand's thirst,
her womb heart's sheath
      to the intellectual thrust,

to rage there
at the edge of the Child.
These are the feard phases of the red.
I had forgotten her.

Towards Whom the procession comes.
The early morning breaks across their way,
the amorous verses fade. In state,
bearing emblems of sexual agony,
vessels of desire, rods of power,
kings and queens
across the green to the Child come.

I had forgot the Lamb.

And have seen a woman where I lookd for Him,
a wounded beast upon the marriage bed
      from which Love ran.

PROOFS

For "wing of the bird" read
    "sing of the verb *part*"
because the clouds departing
    left the look of winter.

For "violet" read "violent"
    following
"The ridges of your face ride
    against my want."

Omit "whatever regret".
    After Chorus II, insert
four lines roman: Do you hear in words
    drifts in the sense shifting,
    teachings that are like birds
    in cloudy speech?

– the fifth line in italics:

A play of birds in the empty sky

Insert "need" after
    "mine is a first song"
For "wrong" read "wring."

    I am tired of the images
that follow me. Delete them.
Don't desert me. You are so far away,
    dear Printer, in another
part, puzzling over my intention
    with cold fingers. Don't

    lose the word ROSE

    isolated on the page.

It is not a flower, but put there
    for an old rising.

YES, AS A LOOK SPRINGS TO ITS FACE

a life colors the meadow.
"This is the place," Abraham said.
The field and the cave therein arose,

even that lies hid in everything,
where nothing was, comes before his eyes
so that he sees and sings
central threnodies, as if a life had

but one joyous thread, one wife, one
meeting ground, and fibre of that thread
a sadness that from that moment
into that moment led.

Poems come up from a ground so
to illustrate the ground, approximate
a lingering of eternal image, a need
known only in its being found ready.

The force that words obey in song
the rose and artichoke obey
in their unfolding towards their form.
– But he wept, and what grief?

had that flowering of a face touchd
that may be after struggle
a song as natural as a glance
that came so upon joy as if this were the place?

It returns. He cannot return. He sends
a line out, of yearning, that might be
in movement of music seen once in a face
reference to a melody heard in passing.

YES, AS A LOOK SPRINGS TO ITS FACE,

as earth, light and grass illustrate the meadow,
there's a natural grace I hope for
that unknowing a poem may show
having its life in a field of rapture,

a book made full of days (pages),
a ready effort full of all places then
that may be because I have loved them
part-song of companions
and of those unknown, alike in soul.

For them may there be a special green
and flowering of life in these words –
eager to be read, taken, yielded to.

Yes, though I contrive the mind's measure
and wrest doctrine from old lore,
it's to win particular hearts,
to stir an abiding affection for this music,
as if a host of readers will join the Beloved

ready to dance with me, it's for the
    unthinking
ready thing I'm writing these poems.

A POEM BEGINNING WITH A LINE BY PINDAR

1

The light foot hears you and the brightness begins
god-step at the margins of thought,
    quick adulterous tread at the heart.
Who is it that goes there?
    Where I see your quick face
notes of an old music pace the air,
torso-reverberations of a Grecian lyre.

In Goya's canvas Cupid and Psyche
have a hurt voluptuous grace
bruised by redemption. The copper light
falling upon the brown boy's slight body
is carnal fate that sends the soul wailing
up from blind innocence, ensnared
    by dimness
into the deprivations of desiring sight.

But the eyes in Goya's painting are soft,
diffuse with rapture absorb the flame.
Their bodies yield out of strength.
    Waves of visual pleasure
wrap them in a sorrow previous to their impatience.

A bronze of yearning, a rose that burns
    the tips of their bodies, lips,
ends of fingers, nipples. He is not wingd.
His thighs are flesh, are clouds
    lit by the sun in its going down,·
hot luminescence at the loins of the visible.

    But they are not in a landscape.
    They exist in an obscurity.

The wind spreading the sail serves them.
The two jealous sisters eager for her ruin
    serve them.
That she is ignorant, ignorant of what Love will be,
    serves them.

The dark serves them.
The oil scalding his shoulder serves them,
serves their story. Fate, spinning,
        knots the threads for Love.

Jealousy, ignorance, the hurt . . . serve them.

II

This is magic. It is passionate dispersion.
What if they grow old? The gods
        would not allow it.
        Psyche is preserved.

In time we see a tragedy, a loss of beauty
        the glittering youth
of the god retains – but from this threshold
        it is age
that is beautiful. It is toward the old poets
        we go, to their faltering,
their unaltering wrongness that has style,
        their variable truth,
        the old faces,
words shed like tears from
a plenitude of powers time stores.

A stroke. These little strokes. A chill.
        The old man, feeble, does not recoil.
Recall. A phase so minute,
        only a part of the word in- jerrd.

        The Thundermakers descend,

damerging a nuv. A nerb.
        The present dented of the U
nighted stayd. States. The heavy clod?
        Cloud. Invades the brain. What
        if lilacs last in *this* dooryard bloomd?

Hoover, Roosevelt, Truman, Eisenhower –
where among these did the power reside
that moves the heart? What flower of the nation
bride-sweet broke to the whole rapture?

Hoover, Coolidge, Harding, Wilson
hear the factories of human misery turning out commodities.
For whom are the holy matins of the heart ringing?
Noble men in the quiet of morning hear
Indians singing the continent's violent requiem.
Harding, Wilson, Taft, Roosevelt,
idiots fumbling at the bride's door,
hear the cries of men in meaningless debt and war.
Where among these did the spirit reside
that restores the land to productive order?
McKinley, Cleveland, Harrison, Arthur,
Garfield, Hayes, Grant, Johnson,
dwell in the roots of the heart's rancor.
How sad "amid lanes and through old woods"
        echoes Whitman's love for Lincoln!

There is no continuity then.   Only a few
        posts of the good remain.   I too
that am a nation sustain the damage
        where smokes of continual ravage
obscure the flame.
                                        It is across great scars of wrong
        I reach toward the song of kindred men
        and strike again the naked string
old Whitman sang from.   Glorious mistake!
        that cried:

        "The theme is creative and has vista."
        "He is the president of regulation."

        I see always the under side turning,
fumes that injure the tender landscape.
        From which up break
lilac blossoms of courage in daily act
        striving to meet a natural measure.

III (for Charles Olson)

                                        Psyche's tasks — the sorting of seeds
wheat   barley   oats   poppy   coriander
anise   beans   lentils   peas   — every grain
                                        in its right place
                                                            before nightfall;

gathering the gold wool from the cannibal sheep
(for the soul must weep
      and come near upon death);

harrowing Hell for a casket Proserpina keeps
                                                            that must not
      be opend . . . containing beauty?

no! Melancholy coild like a serpent
                                                            that is deadly sleep
      we are not permitted
                                        to succumb to.

      These are the old tasks.
      You've heard them before.

      They must be impossible. Psyche
must despair, be brought to her
                                                  insect instructor;
must obey the counsels of the green reed;
saved from suicide by a tower speaking,
      must follow to the letter
      freakish instructions.

In the story the ants help. The old man at Pisa
      mixd in whose mind
(to draw the sorts) are all seeds
            as a lone ant from a broken ant-hill
had part restored by an insect, was
      upheld by a lizard

                              (to draw the sorts)
the wind is part of the process
                              defines a nation of the wind —

      father of many notions,

Who?
let the light into the dark? began
the many movements of the passion?

West
from east men push.
The islands are blessd
(cursed) that swim below the sun,

man upon whom the sun has gone down!

There is the hero who struggles east
widdershins to free the dawn and must
woo Night's daughter,
sorcery, black passionate rage, covetous queens,
so that the fleecy sun go back from Troy,
Colchis, India . . . all the blazing armies
spent, he must struggle alone toward the pyres of Day.

The light that is Love
rushes on toward passion. It verges upon dark.
Roses and blood flood the clouds.
Solitary first riders advance into legend.

This land, where I stand, was all legend
in my grandfathers' time: cattle raiders,
animal tribes, priests, gold.
It was the West. Its vistas painters saw
in diffuse light, in melancholy,
in abysses left by glaciers as if they had been the sun
primordial carving empty enormities
out of the rock.

Snakes lurkd
guarding secrets. Those first ones
survived solitude.

Scientia
holding the lamp, driven by doubt;
Eros naked in foreknowledge
smiling in his sleep; and the light

spilld, burning his shoulder – the outrage
      that conquers legend –
passion, dismay, longing, search
      flooding up where
the Beloved is lost.   Psyche travels
life after life, my life, station
      after station,
to be tried

      without break, without
news, knowing only – but what did she know?
      The oracle at Miletus had spoken
truth surely: that he was Serpent-Desire
      that flies thru the air,
a monster-husband. But she saw him fair

whom Apollo's mouthpiece said spread
      pain
beyond cure   to those
      wounded by his arrows.

Rilke torn by a rose thorn
blackend toward Eros.   Cupidinous Death!
      that will not take no for an answer.

IV

      Oh yes!   Bless the footfall where
step by step   the boundary walker
(in Maverick Road   the snow
thud by thud   from the roof
circling the house – another tread)

   that foot   informd
by the weight of all things
      that can be elusive
no more than a nearness to the mind
      of a single image

            Oh yes!   this
most dear
      the catalyst force that renders clear
the days of a life from the surrounding medium!

Yes, beautiful rare wilderness!
wildness that verifies strength of my tame mind,
    clearing held against indians,
health that prepared to meet death,
    the stubborn hymns going up
into the ramifications of the hostile air

    that, deceptive, gives way.

Who is there?   O, light the light!
    The Indians give way,   the clearing falls.
Great Death gives way   and unprepares us.
    Lust gives way.   The Moon gives way.
Night gives way.   Minutely,   the Day gains.

She saw the body of her beloved
    dismemberd in waking . . . or was it
in sight?   *Finders Keepers* we sang
    when we were children   or were taught to sing
before our histories began   and we began
    who were beloved   our animal life
toward the Beloved,   sworn to be Keepers.

    On the hill before the wind came
the grass moved toward the one sea,
    blade after blade dancing in waves.

There the children turn the ring to the left.
There the children turn the ring to the right.
    Dancing . . . Dancing . . .

And the lonely psyche goes up thru the boy to the king
    that in the caves of history dreams.
Round and round the children turn.
    London Bridge that is a kingdom falls.

We have come so far that all the old stories
whisper once more.
Mount Segur, Mount Victoire, Mount Tamalpais . . .
    rise to adore the mystery of Love!

(An ode? Pindar's art, the editors tell us, was not a statue but a mosaic, an accumulation of metaphor. But if he was archaic, not classic, a survival of obsolete mode, there may have been old voices in the survival that directed the heart. So, a line from a hymn came in a novel I was reading to help me. Psyche, poised to leap – and Pindar too, the editors write, goes too far, topples over – listend to a tower that said, *Listen to me!* The oracle had said, *Despair! The Gods themselves abhor his power.* And then the virgin flower of the dark falls back flesh of our flesh from which everywhere . . .

the information flows
  that is yearning. A line of Pindar
moves from the area of my lamp
  toward morning.

In the dawn that is nowhere
  I have seen the willful children

clockwise and counter-clockwise turning.

From a nexus in the Impossible a tear flows, absurd grief that is a Universe.

Choirs of the Undone come up from the new mathematics. *Let the ten billion years that are likenesses of God be done!* they cry. *In the orders of the Impossible there are already roseate effluvia of the first sound, fluid mountains.* Of *and* Or *are snails, repeat vegetable lessons, roaring a new will that lifts its horns into the heart of Man.*

Where I am only the Possible extends Its commands, a Lord that has allowd me to crawl thru interstices of Earth to restore truth after truth complete statements of my Creator.

This the magician taught: Let the Flesh be given lips that It may talk and be crucified in the Word. When the sky is the sky it is uncertain it is an elephant. When it is an elephant we are uncertain of the sky.

O how uncertain I said Love. I meant houses awaited us in the frozen air, that our chairs and tables were wings of spirit flapping, continually rising, thru space that is a rock; that thru beds of time pushd up into violence, thru sierras taller than centuries, my mouth sought your mouth to find oblivion of me.

How uncertain when I said unwind the winding. Chiron, Cross of Two Orders! Grammarian! from your side the never healing! Undo the bindings of immutable syntax!

The eyes that are horns of the moon feast on the leaves of trampled sentences.

THE STRUCTURE OF RIME IX

The restless one came from the mountain.

My spirit is like a reservoir that cannot draw up its knees. I crave the visible disturbers – lightning, the naked gods, the falling of buildings.

You mean the Fish that sends from the stench of Its decay iridescences of green, lavender, pink, cerulean of Its living scales. And from the white bars of Its skeleton washd by the sea, bleachd by the sun, everlasting tones resound in the everlasting image of the Fish, fins and forkd tails of the radiant.

I mean the dark cold presence of the Fish, alien blessing, a flashing of Night within the night.

For the mountain is below the lake. A language of clouds is salvation that was once of water.

Now the wind comes shaking the windows, driving furies of rain to strip the trees. The down-rushing torrents, the descending ladders! What do I know of the Fish that It is my protector?

My spirit is like a mountain deprived of the sky. I worry the showing forth by Day, craving truth to break from obscurity the old scales, the stars of my crown.

(where thi• has the sound of tree and
thΛ has the sound of nut)

Thi• ever-lasting of thΛ first things. For thΛ sea is *thi•* and clover reminds me of ever. Thi• learning is in *re-* and in *turning* that forms a ring to reach thi• word *thΛ*. Abounding faith for thΛ sound restored.

Cabinet kings call to your castles!

The children build up from the sand renewd fortresses to stand for an hour, the keep delight has in hopeless causeways. Where Galahad of Boy's Mind rides to his Lady. The waves rush in and defeat their tower. It melts in the undertow. Later we see flowers falling from the wet bough gatherd into the skirts of another lady, who stands up into the trembling colors of puberty, sheathed in a cloth of painted buds. Salmon, pearl-white, rose-blush-of-nacre her colors fly.

For the blue wash of sound drawn back to its shores. A shell appears, is rolld under, comes up again the ash Hell shadows, melts and divides into *ash* and *shell* from which the grave black tides of hell recede.

The sound returns in the shell that is deaths-ear of the wave-roar.

The children fall from the limbs of the ash, pearl into grey. O bloody castle that is world's tree! Our flesh melts in the thorns of your crown. Our dust comes to your knees.

THE STRUCTURE OF RIME XI

There are memories everywhere then. Rememberd, we go out, as in the first poem, upon the sea at night – to the drifting.

Of my first lover there is a boat drifting. The oars have been cast down into the shell. As if this were no water but a wall, there is a repeated knock as of hollow against hollow, wood against wood. Stooping to knock on wood against the traps of the night-fishers, I hear before my knocking the sound of a knock drifting.

It goes without will thru the perilous sound, a white sad wanderer where I no longer am. It taps at the posts of the deserted wharf.

Now from the last years of my life I hear forerunners of a branch creaking.

All night a boat swings as if to sink. Weight returning to weight in the cold water. A hotel room returns from Wilmington into morning. A boat sets out without boatmen into twenty years of snow returning.

A STORM OF WHITE

neither
sky nor earth, without horizon, it's
a-
nother tossing, continually in-
breaking

boundary of white
foaming in gull-white weather
luminous in dull white, and trees
ghosts of blackness or verdure
that here are
dark whites in storm.

white white white like
a boundary in death advancing
that is our life, that's love,
line upon line
breaking in radiance, so soft- so dim-
ly glaring, dominating

"What it would mean to us if
he died," a friend writes of one she loves
and that she feels she'll
outlive those about her.

The line of outliving
in this storm bounding
obscurity from obscurity, the foaming
— as if half the universe
(neither sky nor earth, without
horizon) were forever

breaking into being another half,
obscurity flaring into a surf
upon an answering obscurity.

O dear gray cat that died in this cold,
you were born on my chest
six years ago.

The sea of ghosts dances. It does not
send your little shadow to us.
I do not understand this
empty place in our happiness.

Another friend writes in a poem
(received today, March 25th 58):

"Death also
can still propose the old labors."

ATLANTIS

The long shadow thrown from this single ob-
struction to its own light!
Thought flies out from the old scars of the sea
as if to land. Flocks that are longings
come in to shake over the deep water.

It's prodigies held in time's amber
old destructions
and the theme of revival the heart asks for.

The past and future are
full of disasters, splendors
shaken to earth, seas rising to overshadow
shores and roaring in.

It's the universe suspended by the human word,
as if it obeyd our fear,
prediction of world-end,
Lad of the Flood or Fire-Tiger,

what they say afterwards happend, what
happend or will happen . . .

"Geology," Darwin writes, "loses glory from the
extreme imperfection of the record."

OUT OF THE BLACK

Have you never
stood in the teeth of despair, *lo imperador*
del doloroso regno, Lord of the cold shade?
Do you know your huge self
that from the black pit underlies belief
and to and fro upon the earth goes?
Of grief he has a desolate likeness.
Of accusation he has a part, an army,
a lingering of winter submerged in summer.

A multitude go up into His image and splits apart
into a multitude.

For Judas Iscariot
prepares Christ's passion and Brutus
against the thought of tyranny stands.

Four stones
betray the boundaries of the field to the naked eye . . .

where out of sight
the giant dead lie waiting,
moths of the morning.
Time too is crystalline
and the Great Father of Likelihood
lies hid in the hiding place a moment is.

Under the lemon tree
as I drowsed in the sun I heard
Lucifer's Song in Love of His Lord,
fiery essence, the black desolation
ascending thru the created hierarchies
into the light of the Beloved:

O God, from me upward the cry of all grievous being,
a going up of pestilence into the crown,
for I went down into the end of all things
to bring up the spirit of Man before me
to the beginnings of Love.

BONE DANCE

The skull of the old man wears a
face that's a rose from the renewd Adam thrown.
Slack undulations fall,
radiant teachings from the gospel bone,
     fragrance folded upon fragrance,
tone twisted within tone, of gold,
     cream, rose, blood, milk – a ruddy paroxysm
flowering from inertia.

Sweet Marrow,
it's the hidden urgency we beggd to sing to us
that were a gathering of his children, bone
of his bone.

The pungent outflowing of dead mind
goes toward a dry music, a sapless alert
piping in which the stink   sticks, a
carne vale,   the

     old man capering before his makers,
     stripd of idea.

     The Day is my Lord, the Night is my Lord.
     It's fear of the Lord that informs
          courage
     to dance. *Have you? O have you?*
     the old capering papa sings,

     root to the true corybantic,
     Fear of the Day, Fear of the Night?

The old man is a cave of bones.
The old lady's a cave of bones.
Fear mixd with delight is glee-
fully a chalky face with
     bloody redsmeard mouth
     (human eyes

we almost recognize
heads that are drums,
fingers flutes) *heh!*

sings the old destitute – but he's no more than a figure
cast away into an everlasting cartoon of fathers –

have you such
phalanx of fear within the courageous hand that
music writes?

love of the Night, love of the Day?

UNDER GROUND

                                        first
      more-than-fire, then liquid stone, then stone . . .
where there do the dead go?
in utter subjectivity placated that
      turn upon their own steps?

The old folks, no more than
      old thoughts, dressd in full regalia, dried;
hung in thorn trees; potted;
      boxd, the polishd bones cleansed of rot;

honord by verse that preserves
Hippokleas, first of the boys
in the double course at Delphi;

Ford Madox Ford as well; or

Mr. W. H., half in half out of ground,
the double-you that in the ache of Love
      survives,   for Love's . . .
Hate's a monument too! "all happinesse

              and that eternitie
                    promised
                        by
             our ever-living poet
                    wisheth
              the well-wishing"

. .

Go write yourself a book and put
therein first things that might define a world:

There's a great clock upon which the pole star
      will return, turn,
and return. Cheops' stone mountain's
      a lyric gesture. Homer
underwrites not adventure
      but the way back home
before Odysseus may shed
      a life's disguise. Charlemagne

has a tomb in legend no longer intact
    – looted of its emblematic bees.
Enraged Swift
upon his housekeeper's removing a knife
    as he was going to catch at death
shruggd his shoulders and said:
    I am what I am
and in about six minutes, repeated the same
    two or three times.

    On a graph
a regular progression shows white giants, red
    dwarves, relations
    of mass to densities.

In the poem determining the hue of words
the dead also are rememberd –
        There may be
here at the center of a chamber cut out
        of context
cenotaph for Jeff Rall who
        in youth fell
at Dunkirk, because war was more real
        than Blenheim's
in the Village; but the old teaching is
        he each year
closes the year from us and is to be mournd
        by women
openly, and the verse refers to him
        as to a
secret, a hidden liaison with springtime,
an allegiance to the unmentiond, a
        constancy
in avoiding the well-spring in searching for water
        where there was
a star regularly departed from an old alignment,
        not sorrow
nor happiness involved in the kept dimensions

that allow
no continuous coordination of all parts to betray
the still light
cast in the pool to the eye that has not
demanded it.

THE NATURAL DOCTRINE

As I came needing wonder as the new shoots need water
to the letter A that sounds its mystery in wave and in wain,
trembling I bent as if there were a weight in words
like that old man bends under his age towards Death –

But it is the sun that sounds Day from the first brink,
it is the sea that in its dazzling holds my eye.
How under the low roof of desolate gray
a language not of words lies waiting!
There's depth, weight, force at the horizon
that levels all images.

Rabbi Aaron of Bagdad meditating upon the Word
and the letters Yod and Hé
came upon the Name of God and achieved a pure rapture
in which a creature of his ecstasy that was once dumb clay,
the Golem,
danced and sang and had being.

Reading of this devout jew I thought
there may be such power in a certain passage of a poem
that eternal joy may leap therefrom.

But it was for a clearing of the sky,
for a blue radiance, my thought cried.
Sublime Turner who dying said to Ruskin, *The Sun is God, my dear*, knew
the actual language is written in rainbows.

My lovely field! that into the Day comes. The ants who have great works in the earth tend their black cows, a thick scum that devours the juice of the green.

Gopher, that tunnels in the warmth of the breast, has eaten away at the root of the young artichoke. In the thriving

everywhere, pits of hunger!

Infant snails, pearl pure of the first moisture and light, rise from their cradles of lettuce. Morning's leaves eaten away by their appetite.

The handsome builder, under the Permission, has cleard the lower garden. He has cut the yellow trees down. That we could not name, that were in their youth. He has heapd up their swart branches, their gold foliage.

The handsome builder, sun-swarthy, black-haird, has cleard ground at the boundary. He has torn away the purple briar-rose. That we could not name. He has hackd away the briar-rose, the purple loveliness.

In the tall grass, the cat sleeps.

Under the Permission, O yes, under the Permission, at the edges of light, the perpetual thriving, our clearings there – The handsome builder has torn up the pampas grass that was a lord (a tree) of the lower garden –

our dreams, as the cat too, in those casual nests!

Best of ways. That there be a law the Earth gives and the Mountain stand over us, the Valley haunt us, the Shores between elements draw us. Where is thy Jerusalem? Where is Chou perfected? land at the center? So that the stars arrange, named, into guardian orders.

The structure of rime is in the rigorous trees repeated that take on the swirl visible of the coast winds and the outcroppings, the upraised and bared granites that define sentences of force and instrument.

For the melted Earth has gone up out of the Sun into a law that is of stone. And light melodies of the sun – beauty that has shadows, great rests of dark-cast caverns in the living – play thereon.

For the first law, the stone tables of Moses or of Kung, are instruments of a light music, a melody from celestial orbs outswirld.

Aldebaran, El Nath, and the Raining Ones, the Pleiades, in the east, above the dark mountain. Eye, Horn and Heart of the Bull emerging.

And south, Lord over the dark water, the Scorpion entire, that from baleful Antares upreaches into the Scales of the Law. The rage of the heart ravishing or raising up. For the claws of the heart's bale are two points of the beam in Libra. For in french the fléau is a flail from which the scales hang that balance the soul created and its creation.

Best of ways. That there be a law under the stars. For the galaxies drift outward to enter a new universe.

That there be, where we are, a law. And, seeing the mountain, the stream defining the valley, the old sea, we say *This*

is the place.

ANOTHER ANIMADVERSION

And those who tell us Christ was a higher-type man,
model for self-improvement,
spiritually superior to pain,
pretender to the throne that passion is.

For in the poem, the cry goes up:

Love's agony in the deprivation of love
is greater than mine.

Divine Being shows itself
not in the rising above,
but embodied, out of
deliberate committed lines of stone or flesh
flashings of suffering shared.

Transient beauty of youth
that into immortality goes direct,
forsaking us? Aye, but bedded in touch,
ever-rememberd Lord of Sensualities.

Those who are feeble raising feeble Christs,
Those who are kindly raising kindly Christs,
Those who are pure raising pure Christs,

in order to reach Him!

Can't you see how those others, the soldiers
throwing dice for His cloak at the foot of the cross,
the crowd of fellow jews and romans
attending the spectacle,
and His disciples among them,
draw utterly away from Him?

As I draw utterly away from Him?

The old lady reading the doctrine out of Carpenter and Whitman,

that He was the Spiritual Man freed from the bondage of old
    ways,
the not-knowing, the servitude, the crown, the grave-end.

That One! whose likeness we see everywhere bleeding,
or on His first birthday, sucking breast, adored by Kings.
    Death itself raises His legends.

The old lady spirited as a bird in the field chirruping,
    with iridescent glass beads, her quick old hands
    turning over the pages of *Leaves of Grass*,

    "He knew . . . He knew . . ."

    her bird-bright eyes
    quick on the page . . .

It's no animadversion, but an affection.
    Because I see something childlike in her pose,
    her keen eye,
    her handkerchief stuffd
between halves of her bosom.

The inbinding mirrors a process returning to roots of first feeling.

THE INBINDING

In noise the yearning goes toward tones
because a world in melody appears
increasing longing towards stations of fullness
to release from memory a passionate order:

the inbinding, the return,
where certain vital spirits of an eternal act
are bound to be present,
echoes there in octaves of suffering and joy.

The inhabitants of Love, the inhabitants of Light,
that were Eros and Psyche,

that was Christ at the intersection of two lines,
is each melos of the melody, limbs of the tree are

MIRRORS,

high part-voices of the first music,
in a winter nakedness standing up from their leaves,
that once blushd first budding, that put forth
        hints out of natural force
to keep the tips green, fingers at the fresh edge of touching,

: and am now residual bare and black
embracing winter – O hell
is perhaps no more than the naked trunk
        seen as frozen back from its springtide of touching

– as God is a Oneness of all things in turn,
        a Being in touch, so that
in the moving mountain there was a god-ness,
in the sky flashing mirror there was a god-ness,
in the hush of the house where my father died, a god-ness,
        where a likeness of shadow
fell away, residual, from the unlikely brilliance
that enterd and took on raiments of lasting
intimations in the torrents that flow thru the leaves
        that man is a light music,

A PROCESS,

where doctrine against doctrine the noysome poets
babble as if their anger mounting might stand for
one tower of poetry. Let them fall away!
My heart despairs. For the poem
beyond all poetry I have actually heard
has words as natural and expendable
as a cold stream of the first water
thru which rocks of my resistant life
yield to the light cleavages of what seems true,
        white heights and green deeps.

Now let me describe the agony,
the upward toppling from — was it a simple feeling?
into stylistic conglomerations of power,
the devouring giant race that mistakes us
opening certain likeliness
so that the gods that had faces of being
fell apart into one thought

RETURNING TO ROOTS OF FIRST FEELING

Feld, græs or *gærs, hus, dæg, dung*
in field, grass, house, day and dung we share
with those that in the forests went,
singers and dancers out of the dream.
For cradles, goods and hallows came
long before Christendom,
wars and the warblers-of-the-word where

me bifel a ferly, a fairy me thoughte
and those early and those late saw
some of them poets,
a faire felde ful of folke fonde I there bitwene.
For the vain and the humble go into one Man
and as best we can we make His song

— a simple like making of night and day
encumberd by vestiges and forebodings
in words of need and hope striving
to awaken the old keeper of the living
and restore lasting melodies of his desire.

AFTER READING BARELY AND WIDELY

will you give yourself airs
from that lute of Zukofsky?

Yes, for I would have my share
in the discretion I read from certain jews,
not ἰδιώτης but standing apart

from or before, ἰδίω (ἶδος: — to
sweat, of the cold sweat of terror)
that's in the double-play of the mind too:

ἴδιος, separate, distinct, peculiar
(mistrust in order to establish trust,
you must be careful) — but queer,

crossd, athwart, fated, fey
is a man with a quick odd look,
cousin to idiocy, that strains to see.

Uncertainty is root of the gentleness.
As to call some one *dear*
treads close to what we dare not confess

or is misused, fearful
in any case. There's that avid Jewess
combining in the familiar address "dearie"

a careless hostility and affection. Two ways
(the rude force, *twēgen*)
the old battleaxe faces —

that hag grasping, without discretion,
a hold that outrages,
in one gesture to destroy and to retain.

Do not touch.
Forbear if you respect the man!
He who writes a touching line dares over much.

He does not observe
the intimate boundaries of natural speech
– then we in hearing must have reserve.

Poetry, that must *touch* the string
for music's service
is of violence and obedience a delicate balancing.

So, driven close in, to the edge of the Law,
there's this
where I have my good teaching of Zukofsky:

> "That song
>   is the kiss
> it keeps
>   is it
> The
>   unsaid worry
> for what
>   should last."

juxtaposing from H.D., *Sagesse:*

> "Goot, gut and good and surely God,
> and so we play / this game
> of affirmations / and"

of names.

For there is that to which we would give ourselves
wholly.

Certain only of certain things,
of what is discernd, drawn in / with
a sure eye, decided, having

boundary – or does boundless faith
include in a sureness of love
a sureness of lasting love that saith:

Now this outrageous old woman and all of

creation that eats at my heart
shall in the end triumph and not be driven off;

shall claim in the first nature a lasting part;
shall so question the soul with the nature of the sun
that all beings cometh into the great art.

•

Will you give yourself airs
from that lute of Zukofsky?
In comely pairs

the words courteously
dancing, to lose the sense, thus,
and return, thus, in time to see

"God is
"but one's deepest conviction –
"your art, its use'" so the text says.

Where the maker follows with care (with caution)
"all who eat there / inseparable"
the right Maker, the Good, is one

of powers present; the work haunted by the Whole
obeys a predilection for a certain form
that in the crafty mind sets up its poles.

•

Good and bad jews, gods
and *bæddel* mixtures,
dwarves then, twisty-sexd men, cobs

that survive in spite of man's best nature . . .
so Shylock pleads
eyes, hands, organs, pain and hunger

– common life. He laughs, he bleeds,
he turns both ways, he is a man.
He's a troll and shares only the human need!

Shrunken Jehovah, cunning Pan!
("Good People" we calld them – another folk
that work underground)

Of such double-dealings I would talk.
Of these are turnd from hostile threads
the round around of a single rope.

Hermes, a cheat and thief, so it is said,
spited out with Aphrodite, shows
the soul through dark ways indeed,

"an école des Sages ou Mages
as ominous as Ojai".
He's the old faker that haunts the page!

not me! that *other* one whose eyes
squint! psychopompos, undertaker,
Thomas the Rimer, Solomon the Wise.

Mercury, the *Liber de arte chymica* says
"is all metals, male and female";
may be within and without the law, day's

child and night's too; may be jew and gentile,
"an hermaphroditic monster even in the marriage of soul and
  body".
The words in the song are *mercurial.*

The poet's art is one of tact and guile, its boundary
limitless only when it's done;
elsewhere seeming almost to flounder

helpless into meaning, by rime
restricted. How are we to follow?
The song circles. Was there all the time

some good sense, new seed in fallow ground?
The beauty is mind,
a discretion circling round

a containd danger, an impending mystery.
Hate and love may in a song be held
as if they were a scale . . . How well the fairy

minstrel sings of life eternal within his hill,
or, in exile, the Rabbi seeking the word
recalls David singing unto Saul

sang in full faith, and sends into the art we share
a tradition, a caution, a string of the lute
from division and union whereon

this air.

INGMAR BERGMAN'S SEVENTH SEAL

This is the way it is. We see
three ages in one: the child Jesus
innocent of Jerusalem and Rome
– magically at home in joy –
that's the year from which
our inner persistence has its force.

The second, Bergman shows us,
carries forward image after image
of anguish, of the Christ crossd
and sends up from open sores of the plague
(shown as wounds upon His corpse)
from lacerations in the course of love
(the crown of whose kingdom tears the flesh)

. . . There is so much suffering!
What possibly protects us
from the emptiness, the forsaken cry,
the utter dependence, the vertigo?
Why do so many come to love's edge
only to be stranded there?

The second face of Christ, his
evil, his Other, emaciated, pain and sin.
Christ, what a contagion!
What a stink it spreads round

our age! It's our age!
and the rage of the storm is abroad.
The malignant stupidity of statesmen rules.
The old riders thru the forests race
     shouting: the wind! the wind!
Now the black horror cometh again.

And I'll throw myself down
as the clown does in Bergman's *Seventh Seal*
to cower as if asleep with his wife and child,
hid in the caravan under the storm.

Let the Angel of Wrath pass over.
Let the end come.
War, stupidity and fear are powerful.
We are only children. To bed! to bed!
    To play safe!

To throw ourselves down
helplessly, into happiness,
    into an age of our own, into
    our own days.
There where the Pestilence roars,
where the empty riders of the horror go.

FOOD FOR FIRE, FOOD FOR THOUGHT,

good wood
that all fiery youth burst forth from winter,
go to sleep in the poem.
Who will remember thy green flame,
thy dream's amber?

Language obeyd flares tongues in obscure matter.

We trace faces in clouds: they drift apart,
palaces of air — the sun dying down
sets them on fire;

descry shadows on the flood from its dazzling mood,
or at its shores read runes upon the sand
from sea-spume.

This is what I wanted for the last poem,
a loosening of conventions and return to open form.

Leonardo saw figures that were stains upon a wall.
Let the apparitions containd in the ground
play as they will.

You have carried a branch of tomorrow into the room.
Its fragrance has awakend me — no,

it was the sound of a fire on the hearth

leapd up where you bankd it, sparks of delight.
Now I return the thought

to the red glow, that might-be-magical blood,
palaces of heat in the fire's mouth

"If you look you will see the salamander,"

to the very elements that attend us,
fairies of the fire, the radiant crawling . . .

That was a long time ago.
No, they were never really there,

tho once I saw — Did I stare
into the heart of desire burning
and see a radiant man? like those
fancy cities from fire into fire falling?

We are close enough to childhood, so easily purged
of whatever we thought we were to be,

flamey threads of firstness go out from your touch.

Flickers of unlikely heat
at the edge of our belief bud forth.